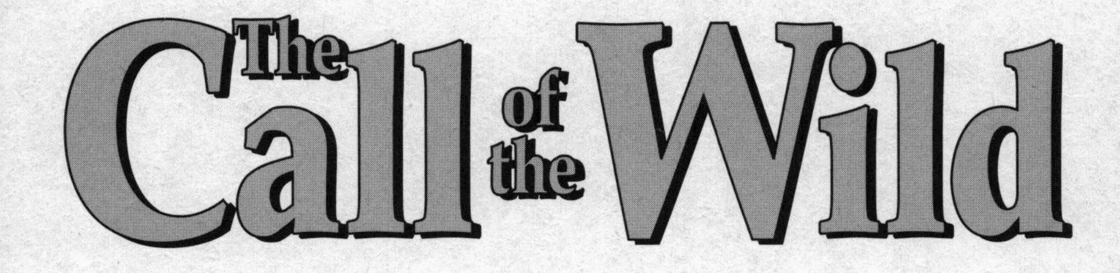
The Call of the Wild

By
Jack London

Adapted by
D.J. Arneson

Illustrated by
Eva Clift

Modern Publishing
A Division of Unisystems, Inc.
New York, New York 10022

Series UPC: 39340

Cover art by Pete Roberts

230 Fifth Avenue
New York, New York 10001

This edition published by Modern Publishing,
a division of Unisystems, Inc.

Printed in Italy

Contents

CHAPTER 1

The
Journey North

Buck didn't know that every dog from Puget Sound to San Diego with strong muscles and warm, long hair was in danger. He didn't know that gold had been discovered in the Arctic darkness and that thousands of men were rushing to the Northland to get it. And he didn't know that those men wanted heavy dogs with furry coats to carry their packs and keep them warm.

Buck lived at a big house in the Santa Clara Valley in sunny California. The house belonged to Judge Miller, and it sat among the trees on a vast ranch, surrounded by broad green lawns, graveled driveways, and stately poplar trees. Behind the spacious house were large stables attended by grooms, a row of cottages where the servants lived, and barns and buildings of every size. Pastures, orchards, and berry patches stretched as far as the eye could see. Sparkling well water bubbled into a big cement tank where the judge's sons swam on hot afternoons to keep cool.

It was here that Buck was born and here he ruled. There were other dogs, of course, and Buck was only four years old, but he had everyone's respect because he was the judge's special dog. While the others lived in crowded kennels or stayed indoors, like Toots the pug, or Ysabel the Mexican hairless dog, Buck had the run of the house and the land. His father was Elmo, a huge Saint Bernard who had been the judge's inseparable companion. His mother was Shep, a sleek Scotch shepherd.

In four years Buck had grown strong and trim. He hunted and ran and loved to swim. He weighed 140 pounds and not an ounce was fat. He carried himself like royalty, for that is what he was in his master's domain.

Buck knew nothing of the Klondike and the frozen North that lured men from all over the world with dreams of gold. He also did not know that Manuel, the gardener's helper, desperately needed money to pay his gambling debts and would do anything to get it.

One evening when the judge was away on business and his sons were not around, Manuel took Buck on a walk through the orchard. Nobody saw them

leave, and when they arrived at a small railroad stop called College Park, only one man witnessed their arrival. He approached Manuel.

"I'd feel better if these goods was wrapped," the man said gruffly.

Manuel tied a length of stout rope around Buck's neck under the collar. "Just give it a twist and he won't be any trouble," he said.

Buck accepted the rope because he trusted men he knew. But when Manuel handed the rope to the stranger, Buck growled to show his displeasure. The man jerked the rope so it tightened around Buck's neck, choking him.

Enraged, Buck leaped at the man's throat, knocking him flat on his back. The man pulled the rope with all his might. Buck's anger flared, but the rope only tightened more. Soon he couldn't breathe. His strength faded and his eyes began to glaze. He fell unconscious to the ground.

The men picked Buck up and threw him into a baggage car.

The shriek of a locomotive whistle wakened Buck. He rose to his feet and stood unsteadily as the floor beneath him jolted back and forth. He knew at once that he was on a train rumbling across the countryside, because he had traveled by train with the judge many times and knew the sensation well.

Buck turned his head in time to see the stranger spring for his throat. Rage filled Buck's eyes. He opened his powerful jaws and clamped them shut on his kidnapper's hand. Buck held tightly and did not let go until the rope around his neck choked him senseless.

The baggageman stepped into the car. The stranger looked at Buck and then at the man. "Dog's sick," he said. "I'm takin' him to 'Frisco to a dog doctor."

In San Francisco, the stranger hurried to a saloon on the waterfront. His hand was wrapped in a bloody

handkerchief and his trouser leg was torn, the result of Buck's valiant struggle. The proud dog was at the end of the rope, still tightly knotted around his neck. The saloonkeeper met the man in a shed behind the saloon.

"All I get is fifty dollars," the stranger grumbled. He unwrapped the bloody bandage and looked at his damaged hand. He glared at the dog. "But I wouldn't do it again for a thousand."

"What did you pay the man who sold you the dog?" the saloonkeeper asked.

"A hundred," the stranger said. "He wouldn't take a nickel less."

The saloonkeeper counted out $150 and gave them to the stranger. "There's a hundred and fifty for him," he said. He glanced at the dog and sneered. "But he's worth every penny." He turned to the stranger. "Now give me a hand."

Still dazed, Buck tried to fight back as the men grabbed him and threw him down, but the rope choked him into submission once again. The men filed the brass collar from Buck's neck, removed the rope, and tossed him into a cagelike crate.

Buck lay in the crate all night. He was puzzled and angry. He could not understand what had happened to him

or why he was penned in the narrow crate. A sense of dread hung over him, but he did not know what it meant.

Each time the door to the shed rattled, he leaped to his feet expecting to see the judge, but it was always the fat-faced saloonkeeper peering in by the dim light of a candle. Buck's ready bark of joy turned into a savage growl.

The next morning four men came for the crate. They were ragged-looking creatures who poked at him with sticks and laughed at his helplessness. Buck

snapped at the sticks until he realized that's what they wanted. He lay motionless as they loaded the crate on a wagon.

The crate was moved by many hands. It was just another large box that went from wagon to ferry boat, and finally to the express car on a train that wailed as it sped across the land. This was the beginning of a long and lonely passage.

Buck lay sullenly in his makeshift cage without eating or drinking. He growled at the men who worked in the baggage car, and they answered his snarls by laughing and teasing. The more they teased, the more Buck's anger grew. Hungry and thirsty, his only consolation was that the despised rope was off his neck.

For two days and nights the train raced north, and in all that time Buck refused to eat or drink. A dark wrath filled him so completely that even the judge would not have recognized him. He had changed from a well-trained animal into a raging fiend.

When the train rumbled to a stop in Seattle, the men on the train were glad to see the crate and its red-eyed captive taken away. The crate was carried by wagon to a high-walled yard, where it was met by a big man wearing a red sweater. The man held a hatchet in one hand and a club in the other.

Buck sensed this man would be his next tormentor. He threw himself against the bars and growled savagely, but the man merely smiled. He jammed the blade of his hatchet into the crate and pried a bar loose. The driver of the wagon and his helpers scattered to safety on top of the wall.

The man chopped at the crate, and each time the hatchet fell Buck charged the splintering wood with his teeth. The moment the opening was large enough for Buck to get through, the man dropped his hatchet and took the club in his right hand.

There was nothing between Buck

and the man. Powered by two days of hate and resentment, he leaped at the man. His 140 pounds burst from the cage in an explosion of growling fur.

The man's club spun at the end of his arm. It landed against Buck's flesh with a dull thump and knocked him to the ground in a heap. Buck's rage was mixed with confusion. He had never been struck by a club before. He leaped to his feet and jumped at the man again, snarling more fiercely than ever. Again the heavy club knocked him to earth, but this time Buck saw what it was. He charged the man again and again, but each time the club knocked him down.

Dazed and staggering, Buck limped unsteadily as the man raised his club again. But this time the blow landed on Buck's nose with a pain unlike any he'd ever felt in his life. His rage reawakened, Buck hurled himself at the man, roaring like a lion.

The man was ready. He brought the club up from below with such force that it flipped the dog in midair. Buck fell in a heap. The man stepped forward and let loose the blow he'd been saving for last. It knocked Buck out cold.

The men on the wall who had watched the horror glanced at one another. "He's one fierce dog-breaker," a man said. The others nodded.

Buck awakened, but his strength was gone. He lay where he had fallen as the man in the red sweater read the saloonkeeper's note that had accompanied the crate.

"His name is Buck," he read aloud. He looked down at the sorry creature at his feet. He spoke in a friendly voice. "Well, Buck, my boy, we've settled our quarrel and that's that. You know your place, and I know mine. Be a good dog, and all will be well, but be a bad dog and I'll knock the stuffin' outa you. Understand?"

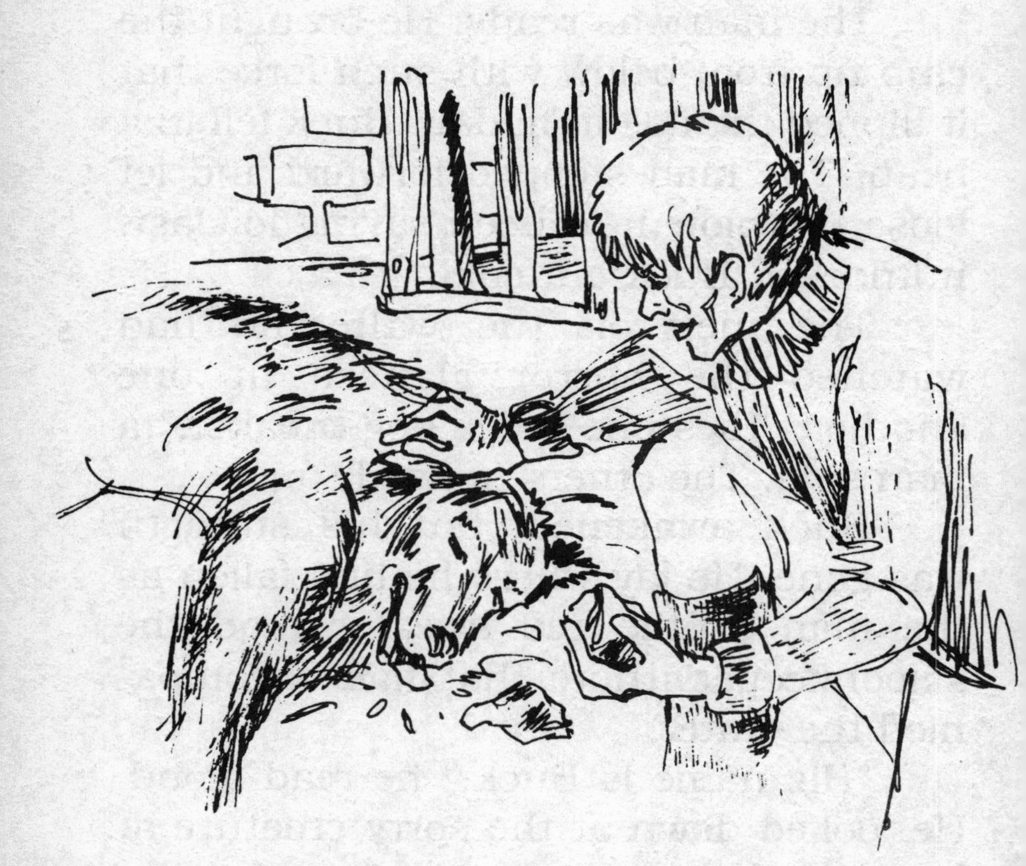

The man spoke without fear, and as he did, he patted Buck's head with the same hand that had held the club. Buck's hair bristled, but he did not protest. The man brought him water, and Buck drank eagerly. A few moments later, when the man offered him pieces of raw meat, he ate them chunk by chunk from the man's hand.

Buck knew he was beaten, but he was not broken. He knew that he stood no chance against a man with a club and he would never forget it. The club was the law.

Over the next few days, more dogs in rough wooden crates arrived, and Buck watched as each one was subdued by the man and his club. The rule was driven home each time he saw the brutal lesson. A man with a club was a master to be obeyed. But this did not mean to Buck that such a master had to be appeased. Some dogs licked the man's hand after they were beaten, and others wagged their tails, but Buck would never do either.

Every once in a while strangers would come. They would talk and argue with the man in the red sweater, but finally they would give the man money

and leave with one or more dogs. They never returned, and Buck began to fear the future.

One day, a little withered man appeared who spoke very little English and had a thick accent. "*Sacré bleu*!" he exclaimed when he spied Buck. "Dat one fine dog! How much he cost?"

"Three hundred, and that's a bargain," the man in the red sweater answered quickly. "And what difference does it make since you're spending government money anyway, Perrault?"

Perrault grinned. He knew dogs and the moment he saw Buck he knew he'd found one dog in a thousand. One in ten thousand, he thought to himself. He didn't argue with the man in the red sweater because he knew that prices for dogs were booming. Buck would make a fine dispatch carrier for the Canadian government. The man selected another dog, a good-natured Newfoundland named Curly, and paid the man in the red sweater for the pair. He led the two dogs away and Buck never saw the man in the red sweater again.

Perrault took the dogs to the harbor, where he boarded the steamer *Narwhal* with them. Buck looked back at the land and the city of Seattle as the small coastal steamer pulled away from its dock. It was the last he saw of the warm Southland. The little man led the dogs below and turned them over to a giant, dark-faced French-Canadian, called François.

These were a new kind of men to Buck, and not the last he would meet. Although he did not develop any affection for them, he did learn to respect them. Buck soon learned that they were fair and impartial when they administered justice, and they knew too much about dogs to be fooled by dogs.

Buck and Curly were quartered in the 'tween-decks of the *Narwhal* with two other dogs. One was a big, snow-white fellow from Spitzbergen, named

Spitz, who had belonged to a whaling captain. The dog had once been on a Geological Survey in the icy tundra of northern Canada.

Spitz was friendly, in a treacherous sort of way. He could smile casually while planning an underhanded trick. Buck learned this about Spitz when the white dog stole some of Buck's food at their first meal.

Buck leaped at the dog, but before he reached him, François's whip sang through the air to nip the thief and punish him. Buck decided that François was quite fair, and his respect for the man grew.

The second dog, called Dave, wanted nothing more than to be left alone. He didn't make advances on the others, and he was ignored in return. He also didn't

try to steal from the newcomers. He was a gloomy fellow who ate, slept, and yawned, but showed no interest in what was going on. Even when the *Narwhal* entered Queen Charlotte Sound and the water grew rough and the small vessel pitched and rolled as if it were alive, Dave paid little attention. The wild rocking terrified Buck and Curly, but Dave merely glanced at them and, with a yawn, fell back asleep.

The ship plowed northward day and night, throbbing monotonously to the steady pulse of its churning propeller. Each day was like the others, although Buck noticed that the weather was growing steadily colder. Then one morning the propeller stopped and the ship was quiet. An atmosphere of excitement spread through the 'tween-decks. Buck sensed it, and so did the other dogs. A change was at hand.

François leashed the dogs and took them above. As Buck stepped out of the hold and onto the cold deck, his feet sank into something he had never seen before. It was cold and white and mushy like mud. He jumped back with a snort. The air was filled with more of the stuff, softly falling from the sky in tiny flakes. Some of it landed on Buck, and he shook himself soundly, but more fell as fast as he could shake it off.

Buck sniffed at the white stuff and tried to lick some from the deck. It bit his tongue like fire and suddenly disappeared. Curious, he licked up more, but it vanished like the first. A roar of laughter went up as the people on deck watched Buck's antics. He felt ashamed, although he didn't know why, because it was his first snow.

CHAPTER 2

The Law of Club and Fang

Buck's first day ashore was a nightmare. Torn from his lazy, sun-kissed life in the heart of civilization, he found himself thrown into an unimaginable savage existence. It was a place where every hour was filled with shock and surprise. There was no peace, rest, or safety. Instead, there was the constant need to be on the alert. Danger lurked in the noise and confusion, and any who dropped their guard suffered the consequences. There was no law except the law of club and fang.

Buck had never seen dogs fight the way the wolfish creatures in this lawless place fought. The first fight he saw taught him an unforgettable lesson. If it had been his fight, he would not have lived to benefit from what it taught him about survival. Curly was the victim.

The dogs were camped near the log store. Curly, always friendly, innocently moved toward a husky as big as a full-grown wolf but only half Curly's size. The husky struck unexpectedly with the speed of a coiled rattlesnake, flashing teeth bared like tiny metal knives. They clamped tightly on Curly's snout and cut her face from eye to jaw.

As quickly as the husky struck, he leaped away. It was the way wolves fought, leaping in and out with startling speed. Instantly, thirty or forty huskies raced to the fight and surrounded the two combatants in a strangely silent circle.

Buck watched but did not understand the silence or the eager way the circle of dogs licked their chops.

Curly did not hold back. She

rushed the husky, but once again he struck quickly and leaped aside. Curly spun around and charged the smaller dog, but this time he did not strike with his teeth. This time he threw himself at the oncoming dog so that his chest struck her sharply with his full force. The unexpected blow knocked the

Newfoundland off her feet, and she tumbled helplessly to the ground. It was precisely what the other dogs were waiting for. Before Curly could get back up, the circle of huskies, now a howling horde of

snarling, yelping creatures, closed in on her and buried her beneath their bristling bodies.

It all unfolded so quickly that Buck didn't realize what was happening. Spitz also watched, but the laughter on his face showed he had known exactly what Curly's fate would be.

François grabbed a club and sprang feetfirst into the writhing mass of dogs. Three other men with clubs joined him, and they all swung wildly at the dogs to scatter them. But it was too late. Curly had been knocked down just two minutes before the last dog was clubbed away, but she had already been torn to pieces. Her limp, lifeless body lay in the trampled snow, unresponsive to the angry curses François hurled at her attackers.

Curly's death and its stark memory burned into Buck's mind so that he would never forget it. That was the way it was in the North. There was no fair play. Once you went down, that was the end of you. He knew then and there that he would never go down.

Buck glanced at Spitz. The white dog's red tongue darted from his mouth again in laughter. From that moment on, Buck despised him with a deathless hatred that knew no bounds.

The shock of Curly's tragic death

had barely passed when Buck got another jolt. François took him aside one day and fastened a strange assortment of straps and buckles over his back and chest. Buck recognized it as a harness because he had watched the grooms put them on horses at home. He had seen how the horses were then put to work hauling and pulling.

François attached the harness to a sled, climbed on, and made Buck pull him deep into the forest surrounding the valley. The big French-Canadian loaded the sled with firewood. When it was full, he drove Buck back to camp.

Buck's dignity smarted with the knowledge that he had been reduced to a common draft animal, but he was too wise to refuse to work. He knew that rebellion would gain nothing. So he bent his back to the tasks François set him to, and did his best.

François was a stern master who demanded instant obedience. If he did not receive it, his whip stung until he did. Dave was already experienced at pulling in harness as the wheeler, or sled dog, who was the first hitched in front of the sled. He trotted right behind Buck and nipped his hindquarters whenever Buck was wrong. Spitz, the lead dog, was just as experienced as Dave, but he could not always turn to snap at Buck. To show his displeasure with Buck's mistakes, Spitz would growl or toss his weight from side to side in the traces, jerking Buck in the direction he should go.

Buck learned quickly from the combined lessons of his two sled mates and François's biting whip. He knew to stop at "Ho!", to go ahead with "Mush!", to swing wide on bends in the trail to avoid catching the sled on branches or rocks; and to run fast enough to stay ahead of the wheeler when the loaded sled raced downhill on the dogs' heels.

"They t'ree vair' good dogs," François said to Perrault. "But dat Buck, he pull like the devil. I teech him quick as anything I see."

Perrault was anxious to get on the trail with his dispatches. That afternoon, Perrault returned to camp with two more dogs, Billee and Joe. They were true huskies, and brothers as well. Even though they had the same mother, they were as different as night and day. Billee was extremely good-natured, while Joe was the opposite, a sour and very private creature with a constant snarl and an evil eye.

Buck accepted the new dogs as comrades, and Dave ignored them, but Spitz challenged each of them in order to beat them soundly. Billee cowered and wagged his tail to avoid Spitz's sharp teeth, but it was no use. Billee howled in pain when the white dog nipped his flank. Joe tried a different approach. No matter how quickly Spitz circled the husky, Joe spun equally fast, so that the two were always facing each other. Joe's mane bristled, his ears went back, and his jaws snapped noisily beneath his gleaming eyes in a dramatic display of hostile fear.

The ruse worked, and Spitz turned

away, preferring to forget disciplining the new arrival rather than face such a terrible-looking challenge. To hide his discomfort, he turned toward Billee, who ran wailing back to the safety of the camp.

By evening, Perrault added one more dog to the team. He was Sol-leks, which means Angry One. Sol-leks was an old husky, long and lean and gaunt. He had a battle-scarred face, and a single eye that flashed a warning that he was a dog who commanded respect. He

was like Dave in that he asked for nothing, gave nothing, and expected nothing. Even Spitz left him alone when he marched somberly into the group.

Unluckily, it was Buck who discovered a peculiar trait of Sol-leks's. The one-eyed dog did not like to be approached from his blind side. Buck learned this the hard way when he unwittingly stepped up to Sol-leks's side the same day he arrived. Without warning, the old dog whirled toward Buck, and with sharp teeth, ripped a three-inch gash down Buck's shoulder.

The harsh lesson was enough. Buck avoided Sol-leks's blind side—and trouble—to the last of their comradeship. Like Dave, the old dog's only outward interest was to be left alone. However, as Buck would learn later, he and Sol-leks shared one vital ambition.

That night, Buck could not sleep because of the bitter cold. Perrault and François's tent glowed like a beacon on

the white plain, illuminated by a flickering candle. Buck slipped inside but was instantly pelted by a shower of curses and metal pots. He turned around and fled back into the darkness and cold.

The wind whipped his fur, driving the chill to his skin. His wounded shoulder ached. He glanced at the tent hopefully, then lay down on the snow. He closed his eyes but he could not sleep. Soon the piercing cold drove him shivering to his feet.

Miserable, he wandered through the camp from tent to tent. Savage dogs leaped at him from the shadows with teeth bared, but he had already learned how to defend himself. He bristled his neck hair and snarled viciously until they turned away and left him alone. Unable to find welcome or warmth, he turned back to his own camp and to the company of his own teammates.

The tent still glowed warmly, but to Buck's astonishment the dogs were

gone. He trotted back, searching through the darkened camp, but returned without finding them. If they were in the tent, he would not have been driven out. But if not there, where?

Buck tucked his tail between his legs, and with his face turned away from the steady blast of cold air, he forlornly circled the tent. Without warning, the snow beneath his feet gave way and he sank to his shoulders. Something wriggled under his feet. He leaped straight up, snarling with fear.

A yelp, muffled by a thick layer of snow, came from the hole he had made. It was friendly, and Buck was curious. He slowly approached the hole and stuck his snout deep inside. Warm air rose from the hole. He sniffed it. To his surprise, Billee lay curled into a snug ball at the bottom of the hole. The good-natured husky whined and wiggled to show he was not offended and even licked Buck's face with his warm, wet tongue to avoid a confrontation.

Buck understood at once where the dogs had gone and how they could sleep in the bitter cold. Confident with his discovery, he found a spot, dug a hole for himself in the snow, and

crawled in. Almost immediately his own body heat filled the space. He closed his eyes and fell asleep.

It snowed all night, and when the camp began to waken and the noise of men and dogs filled the air, Buck awoke with a start. He did not know where he was. He was completely buried in the hole in the snow. Its sides pressed tightly against him. Suddenly, a wave of dread swept through him—the fear wild things have of being caught in the trap. It was not his own memory because, as a civilized dog, he had never felt the trap. But his ancestors over tens of thousands of years had known the fear, and its memory was still there.

Buck's body tightened. The hair on his neck stood on end. He uncoiled his tensed muscles and with a savage snarl sprang out of the hole into the blinding light of day in an eruption of snow. Before his feet touched the ground, he remembered everything that had passed from the time Manuel sold him until now. The camp lay before him just as it had the night before, with dark tents dotting the white ground.

François shouted to Perrault. "What I tell you?" he said with a laugh. "Dat Buck learn queek as anyt'ing."

Perrault nodded gravely. As an official of the Canadian government whose job it was to carry important documents and mail deep into the North country, he was pleased to have the best dogs possible. He was especially glad to have Buck.

Three more dogs were added to the team so that they totaled nine. Perrault and François hitched the team to the sled and immediately set off on the trail toward Dyea Cañon.

Buck was glad to get away from the camp, and though the work was hard, he didn't really mind. The dogs worked with obvious enthusiasm, and Buck felt it, too.

Even Dave and Sol-leks were affected by the change the harness made. Their earlier disregard for camp life vanished and in its place was an eagerness to work. For them, life had no higher meaning than to toil in traces hitched to a sled that they happily lugged over the wilderness trail.

Dave, the wheeler, was first in front of the heavily laden sled. Buck was next, and then came Sol-leks. The others were strung out in a line, single file, to Spitz, the leader.

Buck was hitched between Dave and Sol-leks so that he could learn from them. He was an excellent student, and they were equally good teachers. The moment he made a mistake, one or the other would nip him or give him a shove to show him his error. Dave was fair and wise, while Sol-leks was more physical. And always there was François's whip to underscore the lesson. Buck quickly learned to be a sled dog, and that it was easier to accept the lessons than to retaliate.

By the end of his first day in the traces, Buck had mastered the work. It was a long, hard day's run up the cañon, climbing and climbing until they reached the timber line. There, they toiled across vast glaciers covered with snow that was hundreds of feet deep. Up they went until they reached the great Chilkoot Divide, the mountainous ridge that separates the ocean side of the land from the forbidding, sad and lonely North.

They quickly passed down the long chain of frozen lakes formed in ancient volcano craters and finally reached Lake Bennett. At the lake's end were thousands of gold seekers building boats they would launch to carry them north when the ice broke up in the spring.

The dogs were unhitched and fed. Buck immediately dug a hole for himself in the snow and fell asleep, exhausted from the day's labor.

His rest ended too soon. Early the next morning, long before the sun was up, Buck and the others were hitched to the sled and were soon back on the trail. They made forty miles that day over a trail that was packed and easy. But the next day they had to break their own trail. They worked harder but covered less distance. Usually Perrault

walked ahead of the team, packing the snow with his webbed snowshoes to make it easier for the dogs. François walked alongside, guiding the sled. Sometimes the two changed places, but because Perrault was in a hurry and took pride in his knowledge of the ice, he led most often. Perrault's ability to read the condition of the ice was invaluable, especially in the fall when the ice was a thin sheet over the swift water running beneath.

For days on end, Buck toiled in the traces. Each day was the same as the day before. His masters broke camp while it was still dark and were on the trail before light. By dawn they would already have many miles behind them. The team of dogs would not stop until nightfall, when the two men would pitch their tent and feed the dogs a meal of fish as a reward for the day's labor. Buck would be ravenous, and the pound and a half of sun-dried salmon he was given was never enough. Hunger was his constant companion.

The other dogs, smaller and used to this rugged life, received less food and managed to stay in good condition.

Buck soon learned to give up his civilized manners and to eat like the other dogs. At first he ate at his leisure, but the others, eating as fast as they could, would finish first and rob him of whatever he had not eaten. He could not defend against their attacks, because

while he fought off two dogs on one side, two more would take his unguarded food and eat it before he came back. The answer was to eat as fast as the rest and, when he could, to grab from them what he could. He also learned other tricks by watching carefully.

One day, Pike, one of the dogs, slyly stole a bit of bacon from the men's supplies while they looked the other way. Buck tried it the next day and managed to steal the whole chunk. The

men discovered the theft, but Dub, a dog who was always getting caught, was blamed, and Buck escaped unpunished.

The successful theft marked Buck as fit to survive in the hostile Northland. It was a sign that he could quickly adapt to changing conditions that would otherwise bring swift and terrible death. It was also a sign of the end of his moral nature. The respect for private property and personal feelings he had learned in the Southland was fine where love and fellowship were the law, but in a place that was ruled by the law of club and fang, such civilized feelings were a handicap. In the ruthless struggle for survival, whoever clung to those feelings, whether man or beast, was a fool whose prosperity would fail.

Buck unconsciously adapted to this new way of life. He had never run from a fight before in his life, but the lesson he had learned from the man in the red sweater had replaced his civilized code

with a more primitive one. Before, he would have died if necessary rather than give in, but now, with his civilized nature completely gone, he could easily run and hide to protect his life. He didn't steal food for fun. He stole to survive, and he did it in secret to avoid the rule of club and fang.

Buck's change was rapid. His muscles became as hard as iron, and he grew insensitive to ordinary pain. He learned to eat anything no matter how revolting or indigestible it seemed. And once this food was eaten, Buck's stomach could extract every last bit of nourishment from it to energize him and make him tougher yet.

Buck's vision became as keen as an owl's, and his sense of smell as sharp as a wolf's. His hearing grew so acute that he could hear the whisper of falling snow in his sleep and could tell whether a faint sound meant peace or peril.

He learned to clean with his teeth

the thick ice that formed between his toes. He learned to stomp with stiff forelegs on a thick crust of ice to break a hole so he could drink from the water underneath. He learned to sniff the air to forecast the direction the wind would blow at night. Even when there was no breeze in the evening, he knew where to dig his nest so that when the wind did come, he would be protected.

Experience wasn't Buck's only teacher. His instincts, long dormant, came alive. Generations of domestication fell away so that from vague, long-forgotten memories he remembered how wild dogs ranged through ancient forests in deadly packs, killing their meat by running it down.

Fighting, too, came back. It became easy to defend or attack with a cut, slash, and quick wolf snap the same way forgotten ancestors fought. The memories revived a life within him. That life returned without effort, as though Buck had never forgotten it.

And so, on a quiet, bitter-cold night when he pointed his nose at a star and howled long and wolflike, it was those ancestors who howled through him. His wail was filled with the same meaning they had cast up to the night sky.

Through these ancient songs, Buck returned to his true nature. It happened because men had found a precious yellow metal in the North, and because Manuel, a gardener's helper, did not have enough money to support his family.

CHAPTER 3

The Dominant
Beast

The ancient creature within Buck grew stronger each day, but he kept it secret. He did nothing rash and used his new cunning to his advantage. He did not pick fights and avoided them whenever possible, even when it came to Spitz and the hatred they shared for one another.

On the other hand, Spitz did everything he could to bully Buck and was forever looking for an excuse to start the fight that would end with one of them dead. The end would have come early in the trip if the unexpected had not happened to prevent it.

The men and dogs were camped for the night in a bleak, windswept place on the shore of Lake Le Barge. Wind-driven snow and darkness forced the two men to pick the worst possible spot to spend the night. A solid wall of rock rose up behind them so close to the shore that they had to build their fire on the ice of the lake itself. They had discarded their tent long ago to travel light and only had their sleeping robes for shelter. Their small driftwood fire melted into the ice and went out, leaving them in the dark.

Buck made a cozy nest for himself in a nook in the rock wall. He curled inside it and did not want to leave, even when François handed out the fish he had thawed before the fire sputtered out. But hunger ruled, so Buck ate quickly and returned to his warm nest. A low snarl told him Spitz had taken it over. Buck had let many things pass, but this went too far. The hidden beast inside him roared to life and he leaped at Spitz with

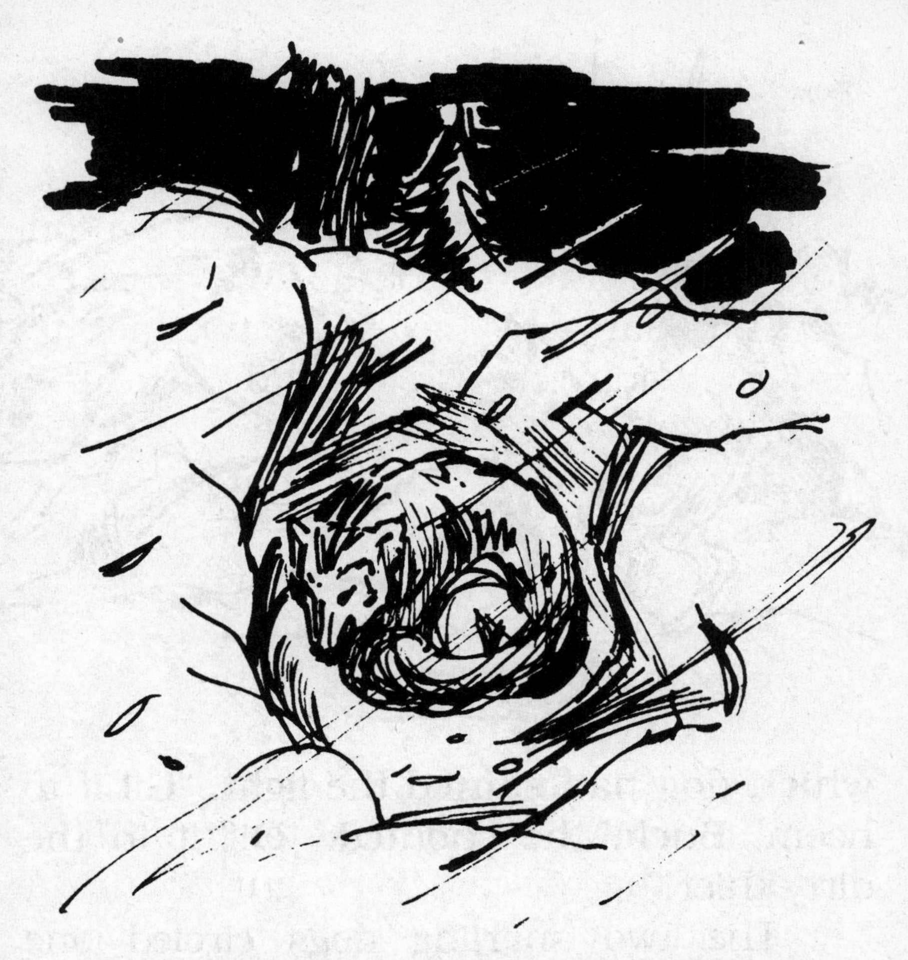

a fury that surprised them both. Spitz was stunned because everything before had told him Buck was a timid creature who survived only because of his great weight and size.

François was surprised, too, but when he saw the two dogs leap out of the stolen nest, he understood at once

which dog had started the fight. "Gif it to heem, Buck," he shouted. "Gif it to the dirty thief!"

The two snarling dogs circled one another, each watching and waiting for the tiny mistake that would give one the advantage. But before it could begin, the struggle that would leave one dead and the other the unquestioned leader was brought to a halt. A loud shout from Perrault split the air. It was followed by the thud of a heavy club, and then by a shrill yelp of pain.

Instantly, the campsite was filled with pandemonium as an immense pack of starving huskies—as many as one hundred—scurried like rats in every direction, crazed by the scent of food. The dogs, which probably came from an Indian village, snarled and fought as Perrault and François leaped among them with clubs whirling at arm's length. The dogs showed no fear, ruled by hunger as they were, and seemed not to feel the blows.

One dog, its ribs showing through its fur, found the grub box and buried his head inside. A solid blow of Perrault's club sent the dog and the grub box flying. Instantly, the pack swarmed over the spilled bread and bacon, growling, snarling, and eating, but paying no heed to the steady rain of blows. The food quickly vanished.

In the meantime, the team dogs had burst from their nests only to be attacked by the ravenous invaders. Buck had never seen such dogs before. They were skeletons with blazing eyes and dripping fangs. Hunger had left them fearless so that it was impossible to oppose them. They drove the team dogs back against the cliff. Three huskies leaped on Buck and in one pass ripped open his scalp and slashed his shoulders. The noise was frightful. Billee cried while Dave and Sol-leks, both bleeding, fought bravely side by side. Joe snapped like a demon, closing his jaws on one husky's leg until the bone cracked. Then Pike leaped on the wounded husky to finish it off.

Buck closed his fangs on an attacker's throat. The fight made him even fiercer, and he quickly sank his teeth into another husky. At the same time, sharp teeth dug deep into his own throat. It was Spitz attacking from the side.

Perrault and François had cleaned out their end of the camp and hurried to save their dogs. The famished beasts fell back. Buck shook himself free of Spitz's jaws. The moment the men ran back to save what remained of their grub, the huskies attacked again.

Billee, driven by fear to bravery, ran through the wave of attackers and fled onto the ice. The rest of the team followed, but just as Buck prepared to flee, he saw Spitz rushing toward him to knock him down. Being knocked down under the mass of huskies meant instant death. Buck braced himself. The blow failed, and he quickly joined the other dogs on the lake. The huskies did not follow.

Later, the nine sled dogs gathered in the forest. All were injured, some seriously. Dub's hind leg was torn. Dolly's throat was wounded. Joe had lost an eye, and Billee's ear was bleeding.

At daybreak they limped warily back to the camp. The huskies were gone, but Perrault and François were in foul moods. Half their grub was gone. The sled lashings and canvas were chewed through. A pair of Perrault's moosehide boots had been devoured, and big chunks were missing from leather traces, harnesses, and even François's whip.

But when François saw the sorry state of the dogs, he turned his attention to them. A fearful thought crossed his mind.

"*Sacré bleu!*" he exclaimed. "Mebbe dose many bites make all of you mad." He turned to Perrault. "What you t'ink, eh, Perrault?"

Perrault shook his head. There were

still four hundred miles of trail between them and Dawson. He could not think of madness breaking out among the dogs. He and François set to the task of repairing the harnesses and getting the dogs ready for the long journey ahead, which was the hardest stretch of trail yet.

Soon they were back on the trail. The white-water stretches of Thirty Mile

River were not frozen over, so the team had to work its way cautiously from one stretch of good ice to the other. It took them six days to cover the thirty miles.

Perrault moved on, leading the way with a long pole to keep himself from plunging into the river when the ice broke beneath his feet. He was used to taking risks, and for this reason the government chose him to be its courier. Each time he or François or a dog fell into the bone-chilling water, the men built a fire to thaw themselves out. Once warmed, the team and its cargo forged ahead until the next ice gave way, or night fell and forced a halt.

All the dogs were exhausted by the time they reached the next river. Rather than rest, Perrault pushed them onward. On good ice they covered 110 miles in three days. Buck's feet were not as hard as the other dogs', and he limped painfully. By nightfall he would drop as if he were dead, refusing even to get up for his ration of fish. François carried it to him and then rubbed Buck's feet. One night, François cut the tops off his own moccasins and made four small moccasins for Buck. They provided great relief until Buck's feet were finally hard enough for the trail without them.

The clash between Buck and Spitz was renewed when Dolly, a quiet dog until now, suddenly went mad. She wailed a sorrowful howl to the sky that raised bristles of fear in both dogs and men. Buck had never seen a dog gone mad, but he sensed the horror and ran in panic.

Dolly, her mouth covered with white froth, raced after him. The two dogs tore across the ice, leaped over fallen logs, and ran as if both were chased by the devil. But it was Buck who was being chased.

François called to Buck to return, and Buck, afraid for his life, wheeled and headed back toward the camp. Dolly wheeled, too, and stayed a pace behind, her teeth snapping inches from Buck's hind feet.

Buck shot past François, who held an ax high over his head. The instant Dolly ran by, he brought the ax down upon her. The unexpected threat was gone, and Buck stood alone, gasping for air.

It was Spitz's opportunity to strike. He leaped at Buck and sank his teeth deep into Buck's flesh. But François saw the incident and quickly lashed out with his whip to drive Spitz away.

"Dat Spitz one devil," Perrault said. "Someday he keel dat Buck."

François shook his head. "Dat Buck two devils," he said. "I know for sure one day he get mad enough he chew Spitz up and spit heem on de snow."

From then on it was war between Spitz, the lead dog and master of the team, and Buck, the strange dog from the Southland. The clash for leadership was inevitable, not because Spitz held

the position, but because Buck wanted it. It was the pride that all dogs of the trail felt about their life—the pride that set them apart.

Buck deliberately and openly threatened Spitz's leadership whenever he could, but the final battle did not come for many days. The team had safely reached Dawson, where Perrault turned over his dispatches and received a new batch to carry back to Dyea, on the other side of the treacherous Chilkoot Pass. After a seven-day rest in Dawson, they set out.

The dogs were in magnificent shape. Their trail was hard-packed by others who had used it since their arrival in Dawson, and Perrault was determined to set a record for the journey. Traveling light, with food deposits placed along the way by the police, the men and team of dogs set off.

They journeyed fifty miles the first day and were booming up the Yukon, a record run already under way. But it wasn't without its problems.

Buck's open revolt for leadership had destroyed the team's solidarity. To Perrault's and François's dismay, the dogs no longer looked to Spitz as their leader, and many challenged his authority. Instead, dogs turned to Buck for protection if caught stealing a fish from another dog. The breakdown of discipline caused quarreling among the dogs. The constant squabbling angered François, who swore and tore his hair.

François knew Buck was behind the trouble, but Buck was too clever to be caught. He easily escaped being punished. He continued to work faithfully in the traces because the toil had become a delight. But what he enjoyed more was to secretly cause fights among his mates, which would tangle the traces.

One night the men and dog team camped at the mouth of the Tahkeena River. Nearby was a Northwest police camp with fifty huskies. Dub, one of Buck's teammates, was poking around in the woods when he scared up a snowshoe rabbit. Instantly, the whole team set off after the startled hare. The huskies from the police camp joined in, and the woods rang with the yelps and shouts of hot pursuit.

The rabbit sped up a frozen creek bed with the pack of sixty dogs right behind it. Buck led the pack but, run as he did, he could not catch the fleeting rabbit. The urge to hunt was strong, and Buck's powerful legs drove him through the soft snow like a whirlwind. His goal was to make a wild kill the way his ancestors had. Sounding the old wolf-cry, he bounded joyfully after the dodging prey, more filled with life than ever before. His true nature was emerging to its fullest.

Spitz saw his chance. He dropped out of the pack and cut across a narrow neck of land separating a sharp bend in the creek. The moment the terrified rabbit rounded the bend, Spitz leaped from the bank and grabbed it in his mouth.

Buck saw the attack and drove himself straight at Spitz with full force. The two dogs rolled over and over in the powdery snow. Spitz leaped to his feet and slashed Buck's shoulder with his fangs.

Buck stood and faced his enemy. He knew the time had come. This would be the fight to the death. The other dogs were silent and watchful. They stood in a rough circle around the two combatants.

Spitz was an experienced fighter who had fought and mastered all types of dogs from Spitzbergen to Canada. The big white dog never acted rashly but instead planned each move and anticipated each attack.

Buck vainly tried to sink his teeth into Spitz's soft neck, but each time he lunged, the white dog met his attack with bared fangs. The dogs circled and whirled, snapping and gouging, but neither could strike a more deadly blow than a cut or a slash. Buck's target was Spitz's throat. But each time he charged, Spitz leaped away. Each time, too, Spitz left his mark in Buck's shoulder.

Spitz was untouched, while Buck streamed with his own blood and panted hard for breath. The circle of silent, wolfish dogs waited in the shadows to finish off whichever dog went down. The fight was growing desperate.

As Buck grew more winded and tired, Spitz became bolder. He charged again and again to keep the big dog from the Southland staggering. But Buck had a rare quality among animals. He had imagination. Not only could he fight by instinct, he could also fight with his head. On his next rush, he acted as if he would throw his weight at Spitz's shoulder to knock him down. Spitz prepared to receive the blow, but at the last minute Buck ducked low to the ground and leaped for Spitz's foreleg, clamping his jaws around it.

Spitz struggled to stand on three legs. Buck attacked again as if trying to knock him over, but repeated his trick instead and snapped the white dog's other foreleg.

Spitz desperately tried to remain upright as the circle of hungry, waiting dogs closed in. Their eyes gleamed, and their red tongues dripped as the circle grew smaller. Buck remained inside the ring, his eyes on his enemy. He circled Spitz, who staggered but did not fall. Buck tensed his muscles for the final assault. Spitz bared his fangs one last time, as if doing so could ward off the inevitable. Then Buck charged. He struck Spitz soundly with his shoulder, and the white dog went down.

The circle tightened around the fallen dog as Buck leaped free. He stood back as Spitz disappeared from view beneath the surge of ravenous dogs. He was the dominant primordial beast, the champion who had made his kill.

CHAPTER 4

He Who Has
Won to Mastership

The next morning, Perrault and François discovered Spitz missing and Buck covered with wounds. "That Spitz fight like a devil," Perrault said as he examined Buck's injuries.

François nodded. "But this Buck fight like two devils," he said. "Now no more Spitz, no more trouble, and we make good time." He immediately began harnessing the dogs.

Buck trotted to the lead position and waited, but François brought Solleks to take over Spitz's position. "Eh, look at him," he said. "He think because he keel Spitz he take de job." He pushed

Buck aside, but Buck pushed right back and refused to budge.

François became angry. "Go 'way!" he shouted. He grabbed Buck by the scruff of the neck and dragged him aside. Then he put Sol-leks in the lead position. The old dog did not like it, because he was afraid of Buck. When Buck returned, Sol-leks quickly stepped aside.

François grabbed a club. "I feex you," he cried. He set off after Buck.

Buck remembered the man in the red sweater. He retreated outside the club's range, snarling with bitterness and rage. François returned to the task of hitching the dogs. When it was Buck's turn, François called, but Buck did not move. He had earned leadership, and he would accept nothing less.

Perrault joined François, and for almost an hour the two men threatened and cajoled, swore and threw clubs, but Buck did not give in. He did not run

away, but stayed just at the camp's edge to let the men know that he would come when they gave him his rightful place in the lead.

Perrault glanced at his watch. They had lost precious time and would lose more if the contest continued. He shrugged his shoulders as a sign of defeat. François took Sol-leks from the lead position and put him in his old place in the line. He threw down his club and called to Buck.

With his eyes bright with laughter, Buck trotted to the leader's position and waited as François fastened his traces. He had won.

Buck soon proved his exceptional leadership qualities were even greater than those of Spitz, whom François believed was the best lead dog he had ever seen. Buck excelled not only in quick thinking and acting, but in instilling a new order among the dogs. They had grown unruly over the last days before Spitz's death, but Buck quickly whipped them back to order. Even Pike, who never worked harder than he could get away with, began to pull harder than he had in his whole life.

The old solidarity among the team returned, and when they moved, it was as if they were one dog and not many. When two new dogs were added to the team, Buck quickly taught them what was expected.

"I never see such a dog as dat

Buck!" François said. "He worth one t'ousan' dollair, by Gar!"

Perrault was pleased, too. They were ahead of the record and setting a new one every day over the hard-packed trail. The sled raced over Thirty Mile River, up Lake Le Barge to White Horse Rapids, and on to White Pass. On the night of their fourteenth day on the trail, they topped White Pass and could see lights flickering below, coming from Skagway and from the ships on the bay. They dropped down the slope to the town, completing a record run that had averaged forty miles a day for two weeks.

The drivers and their team became celebrities, and for three days men admired the dogs and spoke in amazement of the record run. Then one day François kneeled in front of Buck. He threw his arms around the dog and wept openly. He and Perrault had new orders. He turned and was gone, and like others before him, Buck never saw him again.

The team was taken over by a man who was half Scotch and half Indian. The work was the same. Time and again the dogs were hitched to the sled to make the difficult round-trip journey to Dawson and back, although now in the company of a dozen other sleds and teams. It was no longer light-running and record times, but backbreaking toil carrying the mail.

Each day was like the others. The

dogs hauled from early dawn to dusk, when they were unhitched, fed, and allowed a brief time of freedom. There were fights, but Buck established his mastery over the whole pack of more than one hundred dogs by beating the three best among them. Ever after, when he bared his teeth and bristled, the others got out of his way.

At night, Buck loved to lie near the

fire and stare dreamily into the flames. Earlier scenes danced in his mind, though they were dim and distant.

He remembered the judge's big house and the sun-drenched hills, the cement swimming tank, and Ysabel and Toots, the house dogs. He recalled the man in the red sweater and Curly's death. He remembered his great fight

with Spitz, and thought of the good things he had eaten or would like to eat.

The memories had no power over him. They had been replaced by more distant, stronger memories of a heritage that had been reborn in him and made him feel alive.

Sometimes the fire seemed like a long-ago fire in the mouth of a cave, and the Scotch-Indian of the present was like another man who belonged to that same past. That man was shorter, and heavy with hair. He squatted by the fire with a club nearby and peered from the

cave as if watching for danger. When he stood, he leaned forward so that he was never fully erect, but his body was quick and his broad muscles strong.

Buck also sensed things circling the entrance of the firelit cave, creatures with glowing eyes and lips that smacked of hunger. He could even hear the sound of brush cracking beneath their feet as they waited and watched in the dark beyond the fire's glow.

The man and the place were from another time, but they were still deep in Buck's ancient memory, part of a world that had reawakened in him.

The moment the Scotch-Indian shouted his name, Buck would wake up and the present would be real.

Day after day, the mail train of sleds and dogs traveled through the north country. At each trip's end, instead of a needed rest, they were turned around in two days for the return journey. The toil took its toll. After

eighteen hundred miles, Buck and his teammates were exhausted. Buck stood the treatment and maintained discipline among the others, although he, too, was very tired. Billee, Joe, and Sol-leks grew more difficult, each in their own way, but it was Dave who suffered the most.

The driver examined Dave but could find no sign of injury or illness. However, there was no doubt that something was wrong. A sharp movement caused him to cry in pain, and he grew so weak, he began to stumble and fall in his traces. At last there was nothing to do but take him out of the line, because he was slowing the others.

The Scotch-Indian unhitched Dave and led him to the back of the sled where he could keep up at his own pace. Sol-leks was hitched in the position directly in front of the sled as wheeler.

Dave whimpered when he saw what was happening. He could not bear the idea of another dog doing his work. The moment the sled was broken out and moving, he ran to Sol-leks's side and tried to push him off the trail in order to get back into his rightful traces.

The driver snapped his whip at Dave, but Dave did not retreat. He refused to run in the rear on the packed snow, but stayed at Sol-leks's side where the snow was deep, and running was twice as difficult. Finally, however, too weak to break his own trail, he fell behind. He staggered bravely until the next rest site was reached and the train halted.

Dave moved to his spot in the traces and, with his eyes, begged to stay there. The drivers talked of how a dog's heart can be broken if it is kept from the work it loves more than life. At last they decided to harness him back into his place. They knew he was dying and mercifully chose to let him die in the traces with pride. But the work was more than the dog could manage. He fell and was dragged, but struggled back to his feet each time.

Exhausted, Dave slept by the fire that night but could not regain enough strength by morning to travel. The sled was hitched without him. He valiantly staggered to his place, where he dropped to the snow, unable to move.

The sled moved away. Dave howled mournfully as the sled and its team

passed out of sight through a thicket of timber.

The Scotch-Indian stopped the sled. He retraced his steps to the abandoned campsite. A shot rang out, and the woods fell silent. The man returned to the sled. He cracked his whip, and the train moved on. Buck and every dog in the train knew what had happened.

CHAPTER 5

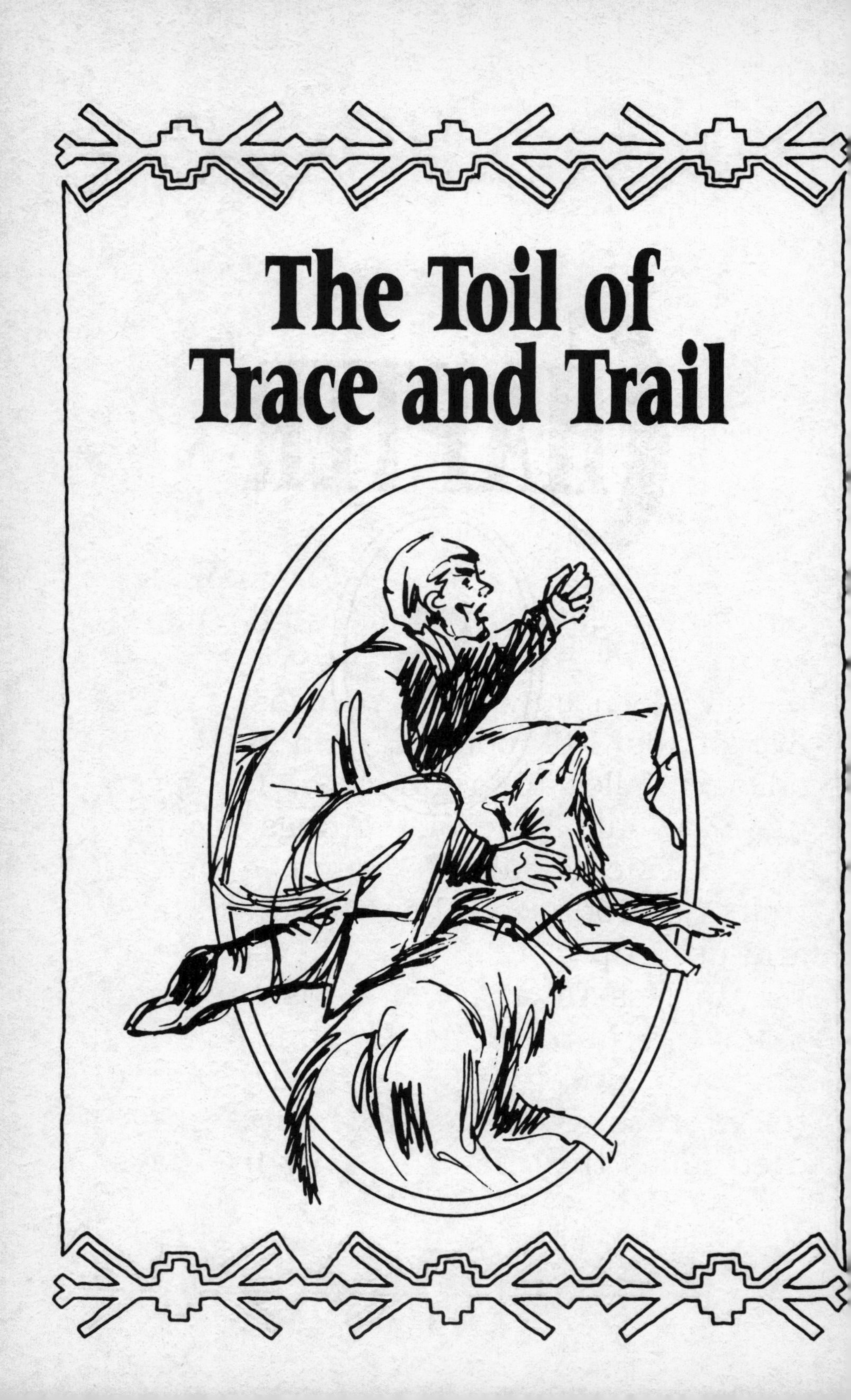
The Toil of
Trace and Trail

Thirty days after it left Dawson, the Salt Water Mail with Buck and his mates returned to Skagway. They were completely worn out. Buck had lost twenty five of his 140 pounds, and the other dogs, smaller to begin with, lost even more weight. None of the dogs escaped the physical damage such constant trekking produced. They were dead tired and used up.

In less than five months they had made the round-trip many times, travelling over twenty-five hundred miles in the process. Over the last eighteen hundred miles they had had only five days' rest. On the trail they could barely keep the traces tight, and going downhill it was all they could do to stay ahead of the sled.

The men expected a long rest upon reaching Skagway, but the North country had filled with gold seekers, and more mail had to be delivered. More dogs had arrived as well, so they were exchanged for the spent dogs, who, like pieces of worn-out, used machinery, were sold.

On the third day in Skagway, two newcomers from the States arrived. Neither man looked fit for the trail. They were Hal and Charles. Hal was middle-aged and weak-looking. Charles, about nineteen, seemed equally out of place. On a belt loaded with cartridges, a big Colt revolver hung from Charles's hip. Next to the revolver was a large hunting knife.

The two men haggled with the Scotch-Indian, who soon nodded his head, extended his hand, and took the money the men offered for Buck and his teammates. The Scotch-Indian left just as François and Perrault and the others did, so Buck and his mates were driven by their new owners to their camp.

The camp was a dismal place with no sign of order. The tent hung loosely, and dirty dishes still lay where they had been used. A woman stepped from the tent. She was Mercedes, Charles's wife and Hal's sister.

Buck watched worriedly as the disorganized trio broke camp and began to load the sled. Though they made a great fuss, nobody seemed to know what they were doing. The tent was folded three times bigger than it should have been, the unwashed dishes were packed dirty, and bundle after bundle was stacked one on top of the other on the sled.

A man from a nearby camp looked in on the disorganized party. "Looks a bit top-heavy to me," he said, trying to be helpful. "Maybe a little too heavy, too," he added.

Charles turned his back on the man and continued to lash the load. When it was done, Hal swung his whip through the air and shouted, "Mush!"

The dogs leaped forward, but the weight was too much for them. The sled did not budge. Hal raised his club, but before he could lower it on the dogs, Mercedes intervened.

"No, Hal!" she cried. "You must promise not to be harsh with them, or I won't move from this spot."

"You don't know anything about dogs," Hal sneered. "They're lazy, and you've got to get tough with them to make them work. That's how they are." He turned to the man who had tried to give advice earlier. "If you don't believe me, ask him," he said.

The man shrugged his shoulders. "They look tuckered out to me," he said. "They don't need a beating. They need a good rest."

Mercedes instantly came to her brother's defense since that was her way. "Never mind that man," she said to Hal. "You do with our dogs what you think is best."

Hal whipped the dogs' backs. They lunged forward, but the sled still would not budge.

The man spoke up again. "I don't care a bit for you, but for the dogs' sake you have to know the runners are frozen, and that sled won't move till you break it out."

This time the advice was taken and the sled finally broke free. Overloaded and top-heavy, it lumbered down the path that was the main street of the town. At the first turn the sled spilled half its load.

Raging with anger at the treatment he and his mates had received, Buck

took off at a run the minute he felt the load lighten. The team raced down the street as more items flew through loose lashes and fell to the ground. Before the runaway dogs were stopped by kind-hearted citizens, the street was littered with gear, and the sled was empty.

People chuckled when they saw the huge amount of unnecessary items the

trio had put on their sled. "If you throw half of it away, you're still carrying too much," a man advised.

Finally, the three accepted the advice of the more experienced. They proceeded to discard half the load, but even then it was sizable once it was tied down. The process took most of the day.

That evening, Charles and Hal bought six additional dogs, all of them newcomers from the outside. They were a mixed lot, and what they knew about hauling and surviving in the North did not amount to much at all.

Buck studied the new dogs with disgust. He would have no trouble teaching them what they should not do, but there was no way he could teach them what they must do. The new dogs were bewildered and broken-spirited by the treatment they'd received since arriving in the North. They had no heart for trace and trail.

The trio began its doubtful journey the next day. The sled was drawn by fourteen dogs, which was more than anyone familiar with Arctic travel had ever seen in one team. The reason was simple. Fourteen dogs could not possibly pull a sled filled with food enough for the team and the passengers. The fact was, the trek began without enough food, though Hal and Charles didn't know it.

Buck resented this journey. His heart was not in it, and neither were the hearts of his fellow teammates. They were all too weary, and the outsiders were frightened. Buck led the team onto the trail, but he did not like it.

Within days it was clear the trip was a disaster. The trio could not make a proper camp, did not know how to distribute the food effectively to make it last, and quarreled among themselves. They were making dangerously poor time and were soon on short rations. Hal cut the dogs' rations to the point that they were seriously underfed, a sure way to reduce the already shortened travel he counted on each day. Neither of the men knew how to work the dogs any better than they knew how to work themselves.

The dogs grew thinner and weaker with every day. When a dog could no longer pull, his days were numbered. Dub was first to go. Unable to pull because of an injured shoulder that could not heal without rest, Hal shot him with his Colt. Starvation soon took the ones who had not learned to survive the way Buck and the others had.

Charles, Hal, and Mercedes constantly bickered over trivial things as well as more serious matters such as gathering firewood. The trip became a nightmare for Buck. When the food finally ran out, the dogs were fed bits of dried horsehide that an Indian had traded to Hal for his pistol. The dogs ate it because that's all there was.

Buck staggered at the head of his bedraggled team, barely able to pull. His once glossy coat hung lifeless against his skeleton-like sides, caked with dried blood from beatings by Hal's ever-present club. His muscles were wasted away to knotty strings, so much so that his ribs showed through the loosely hanging skin. Only his bold heart remained unbreakable. The man in the red sweater had proven that.

The other dogs were in equally bad shape. The whole team was nothing more than a line of plodding skeletons, overwhelmed by misery and no longer sensitive to the sting of the lash or blow of the club. When they stopped, they dropped in their traces as if dead and only rose again when the club or whip beat them to their feet. They staggered on as best they could.

One day Billee fell and could not get up. Hal no longer had his pistol, so he hit the quivering dog on the head with an ax and threw his body to the side of the trail. Buck and the others watched, and they knew that the same fate awaited them. Koona went the next day, but Joe, Pike, Sol-leks, Teek, and Buck pulled on. Discipline among the dogs was no longer a problem for Buck. It was all he and his mates could do to stay on the trail.

The weather was glorious, although none in the grim troop knew it. The days grew longer and the weather warmer as spring worked its way north. Beauty lay on every side, but the two men, the woman, and the struggling dogs saw none of it. They continued their hopeless trek down the Yukon, which was coming to life beneath their feet. The thaw was setting in, and here and there sections of ice broke away to reveal the torrent below.

Unexpectedly, the pitiful collection of dogs and humanity stumbled into John Thornton's camp at the mouth of the White River. The instant they stopped, the dogs fell to the snow as if dead. Charles sat heavily on a log while Mercedes, sitting on the sled with tears in her eyes, watched Hal approach John Thornton.

Thornton was whittling an ax handle from a stout piece of birch. "The river ice is about rotted through," he said after a pause. "My advice is to get off it while the getting's good."

Hal smirked. "That's what they told us before," he said. "Told us we couldn't make it to the White River, too. But here we are." He sat back and pushed forth his chest in triumph.

"They were right," John Thornton said. "Only fools with blind luck would try it, so I guess that's what you are." He glanced toward the river. "I wouldn't risk my life on that ice for all the gold in Alaska," he added.

Hal rose and turned toward the sled. "That's because you're not a fool, I suppose," he shot back at Thornton. "All the same, we'll get to Dawson." He uncoiled his whip and shouted at the dogs. "Get up, Buck. Get up! Mush on!"

Thornton said nothing but went on whittling. He knew it was pointless to argue with fools, and two or three less fools in the world wouldn't change much, anyway.

The team did not get up. Hal beat them mercilessly with his whip. John

Thornton bit his lip at the sight. At last, Sol-leks crawled to his feet. Teek followed, and then Joe rose, yelping in pain. Pike tried, but fell when half up off the ground. Finally he was on his feet.

But Buck did not move. He lay where he had fallen. Hal whipped him with the lash, but its sting had no effect. Buck didn't whine or struggle, but lay in his traces absorbing the blows.

John Thornton rose. Tears welled in his eyes as he paced back and forth listening to Hal vent his rage on Buck.

Buck still did not move. He had sensed the rotten river ice beneath his feet, and he was filled with a sense of impending doom. The blows continued to fall, but they no longer hurt. He grew numb as his life's spark began to flicker. He knew he was being beaten, but it seemed to be far away, and his body seemed no longer his own.

With a sudden wild cry like an uncaged animal, John Thornton leaped forward. He grabbed Hal and threw

him backward. Mercedes screamed, and Charles watched, but neither moved.

John Thornton stood over Buck, too enraged to speak. At last he regained enough control to form the words he'd been thinking. He turned to Hal, who was wiping blood from his mouth. "If you strike that dog again, I'll kill you," he said in a voice choked with emotion.

"It's my dog," Hal shot back. "Get out of my way. I'm going to Dawson."

Thornton stood between Hal and Buck. He had no intention of moving. Hal drew his long hunting knife, but before he could make another move, John Thornton smashed his ax handle against the man's knuckles and the knife fell to the ground. Thornton picked it up and cut Buck's traces.

Hal sheepishly went to the sled. He had no more fight left inside him. He mushed the dogs slowly toward the river.

Buck turned his head at the sound. Pike was at the lead, followed by Joe and Teek, while Sol-leks was at the wheel. The dogs limped and staggered as they pulled the sled onto the ice. Mercedes rode on top, and Hal and Charles stumbled alongside.

Buck and Thornton watched the sled grow smaller as it moved farther and farther up the river. Suddenly, the rear of the sled dropped, the front rose into the air, and in less than a second the whole thing fell through a hole in the ice and disappeared—dogs, people, and all.

John Thornton and Buck looked at one another. "You poor devil," Thornton said. And Buck licked his hand.

CHAPTER 6

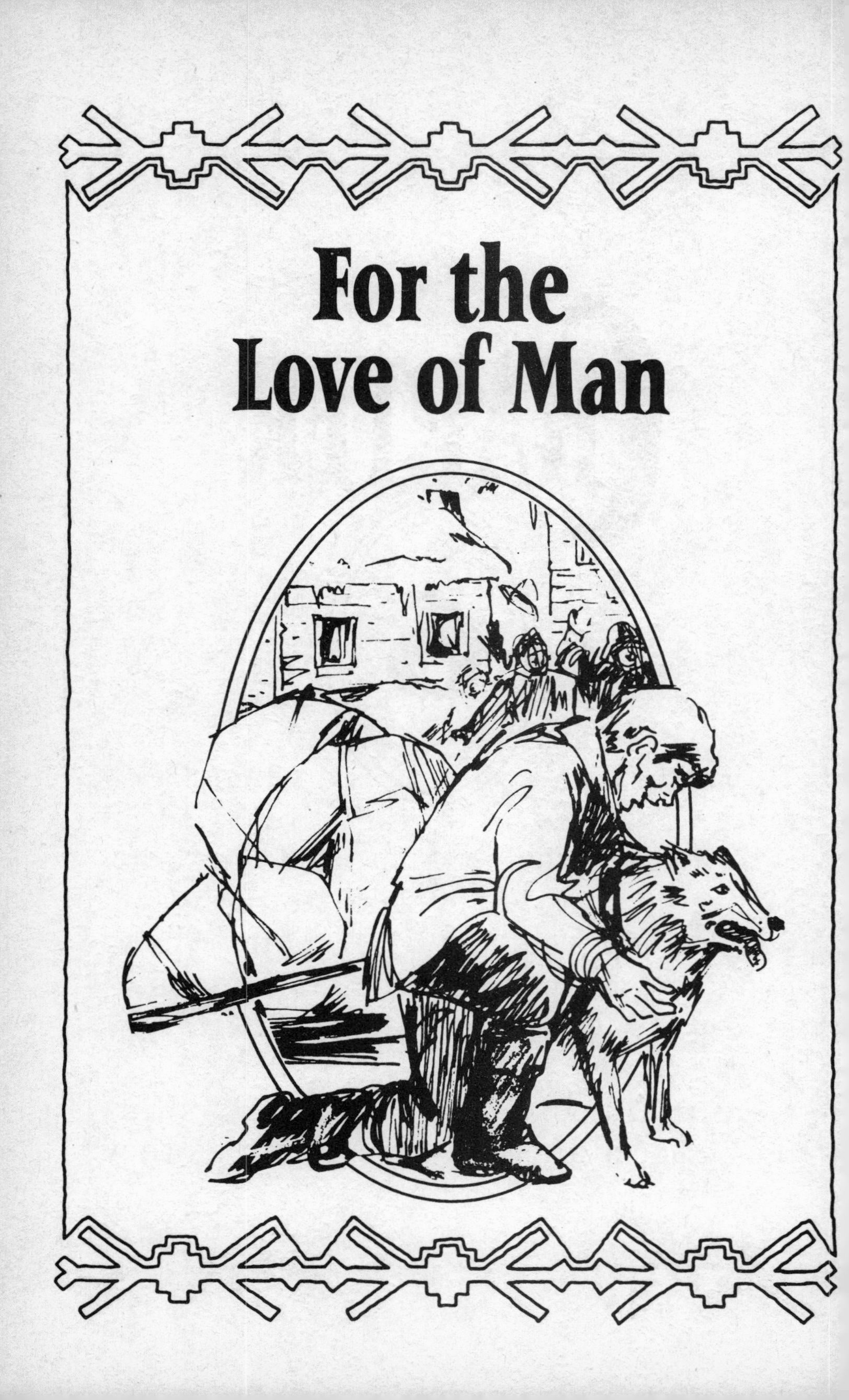
For the
Love of Man

John Thornton's feet had frozen the previous December. His partners had made a camp for him and left him alone to recover while they went upriver to get a raft of logs to float to Dawson. Thornton was still limping when Buck joined him, but as spring advanced and the weather warmed, both man and dog recovered their health and strength.

Buck reveled in this chance to be lazy, after traveling three thousand miles. His wounds healed, his muscles grew strong, and his body filled out to the size it used to be. Thornton and his dogs, Skeet and Nig, loafed, too, as they

waited for the raft that would carry them to Dawson. Skeet was an Irish setter who had taken on the job of nursing Buck when he first arrived. She licked his wounds the way a cat washes her kittens. Nig, a huge, mixed bloodhound and deerhound, was just as friendly, although he left the nursing to Skeet.

The dogs were not at all jealous of Buck. Like their master, they showed kindness and compassion. When Buck was strong enough, the three rollicked together in joyous games. John Thornton joined in with great enthusiasm.

It was the first time in his life that Buck ever knew true love. His relationship with the judge and his sons was a working partnership between a dog and his masters. Their friendship was real, but dignified and stately. Here, with John Thornton, the relationship was one of genuine love.

Thornton not only had saved Buck's life— he was an ideal master. Others who cared for their dogs did so out of a sense of duty, but John Thornton did so out of love, as if the dogs were his own children. He rubbed Buck's ears playfully and often put his head against Buck's while murmuring words that Buck

understood to be expressions of love. Buck adored it when Thornton shook him roughly and then let go. He would leap with joy into the air with laughing eyes, begging for more. "It's almost as if you could speak," Thornton said with awe.

Buck displayed his affection with a bite that stopped just short of pain. He would grip Thornton's hand tightly in his mouth until his teeth left marks, but Thornton knew it was a sign of love and did not mind. But usually, Buck showed his affection from a distance. While the other dogs nudged their noses into Thornton's hand until he gave in and petted them, Buck stood apart, gazing at his master with inexpressible adoration.

When John Thornton sensed the power of Buck's gaze, he would turn to him and, without speaking, return the love with the light of his eyes. For a long time after his rescue, Buck would not let Thornton out of his sight, because deep within, he feared that he would go the way of his earlier masters.

But Buck felt other urges, too. The Southland was gone from his life and in its place was the presence of the wild animal that had slept so long within him. He had learned the law of club and fang well, and he knew he had to master or be mastered, kill or be killed, eat or be eaten—that was the law; there was no middle ground.

As he sat by John Thornton's fire, broad-breasted, white-fanged and long-haired, there lingered inside him the shadows of all the dogs, half-wolves, and wild wolves that had gone before him. They tasted the meat he ate, smelled the same smells, and heard the sounds that touched his ears. And each day their presence grew stronger.

Deep in the forest a call was sounding, and Buck heard it. It was mysterious and luring, and when he heard it he would turn his back on John Thornton's fire and plunge into the forest to find it. Only his love for John Thornton was strong enough to draw

him back. John Thornton, and John Thornton alone, of all mankind, was his master.

Hans and Pete, Thornton's partners, arrived on the long-awaited raft, and the whole party floated on to Dawson. Buck's love for his master grew with every day, and by summer it was boundless. There was nothing he would

not do for John Thornton, and he proved it many times.

Once, in a bar in Circle City, an evil-tempered brute named Black Burton picked a fight with a newcomer from the south. Thornton stepped between them to prevent the fight. Burton threw his fist at Thornton and knocked him backward.

Buck, who had been lying in a corner watching his master's every move, leaped straight at the man with his jaws open, ready to defend Thornton. The bully threw up his arm, and Buck's sharp teeth closed around it. Buck let go of the arm and struck at the man's throat. This time the man could not block the dog's attack.

The crowd pulled Buck off, and a surgeon managed to stop Burton from bleeding to death. A meeting was called, and Buck was left blameless, for everyone agreed that Burton had started the incident. From that day on, Buck's name

and reputation spread to every camp across the Northland.

Buck saved Thornton's life again later that year. Thornton and his partners were easing a boat through a bad stretch of rapids on Forty Mile Creek. Thornton poled the boat while Hans and Pete checked its movement with a taut line from shore. Suddenly, the boat flipped over, and Thornton was pitched into the raging rapids. He was carried swiftly toward a stretch of wild water and certain death.

Buck leaped into the raging water and swam furiously for Thornton. Buck overtook the floundering man, who grabbed the dog's tail and held on tightly as Buck turned toward shore. But the current was too swift, and the two were dragged over rough rocks toward the maelstrom below. Thornton grabbed a rock and let go of Buck's tail. He knew they could not reach the safety of shore. "Go, Buck," he shouted over the thundering roar of water.

Buck was swept downstream. Thornton shouted again, and Buck, glancing back for an instant, turned toward shore. With life-or-death effort, he swam close enough for Pete and Hans to pull him to safety. They immediately tied a line around Buck's shoulders, and the dog leaped back into the torrent.

Again, he swam boldly, this time not for his own life but for his master's. But the current swept him past the man who struggled to hold on to the slippery rocks. There was very little time left before Thornton would weaken and vanish forever.

Buck regained the shore with the help of the rope pulled by the frantic men. Half-drowned, but spurred on by Thornton's faint calls for help, Buck ran upstream and leaped back into the water. The current carried him straight to Thornton, who grabbed Buck before he was swept by a second time. The line tightened, and the men onshore hauled the two over sharp rocks and raging water to shore. They set up camp and did not leave until Buck's broken ribs and Thornton's bruises healed.

Buck proved his dedication and his prowess again later that winter. His name was already high on the totem pole of Alaskan fame, but this exploit raised it to the top.

Thornton and his partners wanted to explore the eastern regions where miners had not yet ventured. But they needed an outfit and had no money to buy the necessary supplies. Thornton overheard some men in the Eldorado Saloon bragging about their dogs and he joined in.

When one man, a wealthy man called Matthewson, said his dog could start a sled carrying seven hundred pounds and walk off with it, Thornton said, "Pooh! Buck can start a thousand pounds!"

It was all Matthewson needed to make a bet. "I've got a thousand dollars that says he can't," Matthewson said, slamming a sack of gold dust the size of a sausage onto the bar.

Thornton knew his bluff had been called. Worse, he knew he and his partners did not have the thousand dollars to match Matthewson's bet. Luckily, a friend agreed to lend Thornton a thousand dollars, though he, like all the others, doubted any dog's ability to start a thousand-pound sled.

The men poured out of the bar onto the ice-covered street. Soon a crowd of hundreds had gathered to watch the contest. A large sled loaded with a thousand pounds of flour already stood on the street, its runners frozen solidly into the ice.

An argument over whether the runners could be broken free before Buck started to pull ended with the decision to leave them as they were. The betting climbed as Matthewson, sensing an easy win, raised the ante to three to one. The winner would receive three times the amount bet by the loser.

Thornton, caught up in the fever of the betting, called his partners. They could only raise another two hundred dollars among them, but they made the bet.

Buck was hitched to the sled. He looked magnificent. His coat was glossy and bright, his muscles as strong as

iron. The bettors realized he was more of a dog than they imagined, and the odds dropped to two to one.

Thornton stepped to Buck's side, but Matthewson protested. "You must stand off," he said.

Thornton kneeled at Buck's side. He put his mouth to the dog's ear. "As you love me, Buck. As you love me," he whispered.

Thornton stood up and put his mittened hand between Buck's powerful jaws. The dog clenched his master's hand tightly. The crowd murmured at the mystery shared by dog and man. Thornton stepped back. The crowd tensed. "Now, Buck!" Thornton called.

Buck moved forward just enough to tighten the traces the way he had learned. “Gee!” Thornton shouted. Buck swung hard to the right with a sudden jerk that caused the sled to groan. “Haw!” Thornton commanded. Buck jerked to the left, and this time the ice beneath the runners creaked and then gave way. The sled was broken out.

"Now, MUSH!" Thornton yelled. Buck threw himself forward. The traces tightened until they quivered. Buck's muscles knotted. He put his head low to the ground and began to pull. His feet clawed the ground, throwing showers of hard-packed snow behind them.

The sled shuddered and then slowly started forward. Buck slipped but quickly recovered his footing, and the sled

lurched on. It moved half an inch at a time, then an inch, and then began to slide smoothly over the ice. It didn't stop until Buck had reached the pre-marked finish line.

Thornton threw his arms around Buck and hugged him. His eyes were filled with tears. A man in the crowd

shouted, "I'll give you a thousand for him in gold right now, sir. Twelve hundred!"

Thornton rose to his feet and wiped his eyes. He turned to the man. "You, sir, can go to the devil!"

Buck seized Thornton's hand in his jaws and held on tight as John Thornton shook him playfully back and forth. The crowd watched in silent awe. They did not dare come forward and interrupt the mystery they were witnessing.

CHAPTER 7

The Sounding of the Call

John Thornton and his partners bought the supplies they needed with the money Buck had won for them and set off after a fabled lost mine, the Lost Cabin. If it existed, they were determined to find it.

The men and dogs moved deep into the untouched reaches of the wilderness, living off the land like the Indians. Sometimes they ate well, and other times they starved, but to them it was all the same. The months passed, but no sign of the Lost Cabin and its treasure was found.

Spring came, and with it a marvelous discovery. It was not the Lost Cabin, but a stream littered with gold. The men worked the stream until they had moosehide bags filled with the precious stuff. After months of hauling, there was nothing for the dogs to do, so they lay lazily about the camp as the men toiled in the stream.

The earlier visions of an ancient time returned more frequently to Buck as he mused by the fire. And with these visions came a familiar sound. It was a distant call from the depths of the forest that aroused intense curiosity and strange desires. Sometimes he would get up from his place at the fire and wander into the forest, but return without learning what he was looking for.

Buck's journeys into the forest grew more frequent as the call grew stronger. He would leave the camp and spend days at a time romping through the woods, watching for signs of other creatures and listening to the sounds of nature.

One night the urge was sudden. He leaped from the fire and ran silently into the woods. But this time the call was not something he heard deep inside. It was a cry as real as the chilly wind, and he was compelled to follow it. He stopped at a clearing.

On the opposite side, with nose pointed skyward, was a long, lean wolf howling toward heaven.

Although Buck had not made a sound, the wolf stopped its call. Buck entered the clearing, careful that his every move displayed friendliness and not danger. But the wolf fled at his sight.

Buck raced after him, and the two ran headlong through the forests, one leading, the other following. Finally the wolf stopped. He spun around and, with fangs glistening, snapped sharply at Buck.

Buck did not attack. He circled the wolf slowly, still showing friendly advances. The wolf watched, but fled once again, and the chase resumed.

Buck overtook the wolf again and again, but each time the wolf raced away. At last, sensing that Buck posed no danger, the wolf let Buck join him.

Soon they were romping side by side as friends. They ran through the night toward a place that the wolf knew and Buck could only sense. But Buck was glad to follow, because it was this place from which the call had come to him so many times. It was *the call of the wild.* Old memories stirred inside him. He felt he had done these things before and that now, with the wolf at his side, he was back to do them again.

They stopped for a drink, and suddenly Buck remembered John Thornton. The wolf started off, but Buck stayed back. The wolf returned to sniff noses. Buck turned and trotted back from where he had come. The wolf ran at his side for half an hour, whining faintly, but finally turned around, and the two parted.

Buck didn't leave camp again for two days and refused to let John Thornton out of his sight. But the distant call returned, and Buck could not ignore it. He returned to the woods, where he stayed for many days.

The wild brother never returned, but Buck did not give up listening for him. He fished for salmon, caught small game, and traveled for many miles, roaming the broad wilderness. He learned fast to dwell in the wild.

Buck carried himself proudly. The size and weight he had inherited from his Saint Bernard father combined readily

with the cunning and intelligence he had inherited from his shepherd mother. The result was a magnificent animal unlike any other that roamed the wild.

"Never was there such a dog," John Thornton said, when Buck returned to camp. Thornton did not recognize the deep change taking place in Buck's nature. He did not know about Buck's secret life, where Buck hunted and lived in answer to a mysterious call.

Fall came, and Buck continued his hunt. He chanced upon a herd of moose. Eyeing its chief, a beast over six feet tall with a spread of antlers seven feet from tip to tip, Buck determined to make the biggest kill of his life. He stalked the herd for days.

The chief, wounded earlier by an Indian's arrow that he still carried in his shoulder, slowly dropped away from the herd. Buck never left his prey, but relentlessly pursued him until, at last, the two met face-to-face.

Buck waited and watched, and when the time was right, he struck. The huge beast went down.

This attack raised his awareness of the deeper stirrings within him.

After a refreshing rest, he turned back toward camp and John Thornton,

which were many miles away. He loped through the forest hour after hour, heading for home with the certainty of a compass needle.

But as he drew closer, he began to feel a dark dread that made him shudder. Buck's senses became razor sharp.

Something had happened in the forest, but he did not know what.

A pungent scent tugged at Buck's nose, and he turned toward it. He found Nig lying in a thicket, dead, with an arrow protruding from his side. A short

distance beyond lay another dog, still shivering in its death throes. The sound of a sing-song chant gripped his attention, and he hurried past, still headed for the camp.

At the edge of the clearing he found Hans, also dead, filled with arrows jutting out like porcupine quills. Overpowering rage swept over Buck. He growled ferociously and raced headlong into the camp.

Buck plunged into the band of marauding Yeehat Indians still celebrating their raid. He leaped at one Indian, the chief. Buck's jaws closed on the man's throat and left the man lifeless. He struck another without pause or fear of the arrows and spears hurled his way.

The Indians could not hit the fearless animal spinning like a whirlwind in their midst. Suddenly, seized with panic, they screamed in terror as they ran into the woods to avoid the evil spirit that had burst upon them in the form of a

raging dog. They scattered and dared not return.

Buck found Pete still in his blankets where he had been killed in the surprise attack. He located John Thornton's scent and followed it to the edge of a deep pool. John Thornton was dead.

Buck brooded by the pool all day. When night came, he began to stir with the new life he had found in the forest. He stood and listened. Faint, sharp yelps called from far away. The memories of his ancient world returned. It was the call, and he was ready to obey. He had killed a man and John Thornton, his master, was dead. The last ties were broken. Buck was no longer bound by the claims of man.

A wolf pack entered the clearing where Buck stood, waiting. Their awe of the bold, silent dog was brief. The boldest wolf leaped at Buck, but Buck struck first, breaking the attacker's neck. He stood over the body as three others jumped at him. One after the other they fell back, cut and bleeding from Buck's fierce fangs.

The rest of the pack joined the melee. Gnashing and snapping, often on his hind legs, Buck fought them off. He was quicker and more deadly than any, and none could get close enough to drop him. He raced back and forth to prevent an attack from behind, finally retreating to the river, where he placed himself on the bank. Protected on three sides, he faced his attackers.

The wolves struck at him over and over, but he drove them back each time. Their ferocity was no match for his, and soon they began to drop out of the fight, their tongues flopping from their mouths in exhaustion. Soon they all stopped and were content to watch.

One wolf, long and lean and gray, advanced cautiously. Buck recognized him. It was the wild brother he had run with for a night and a day. The two whined and touched noses.

An old wolf, scarred by earlier battles, came forward. After Buck sniffed noses with him, the old wolf sat down and pointed his nose at the moon. He let out a long wolf howl that was quickly joined by the others.

The call came to Buck, who sat and howled with them. The pack crowded around him, sniffing. Then the leaders sprang away to the woods, and the pack followed. Buck ran with them, side by side with the wild brother, yelping as he ran.

It was not many years later that the Indians noticed a change in the timber wolves roaming the forests. Some had new markings never before seen. Some had splashes of brown on their heads and muzzles, with a rift of white fur down their chests.

The Indians tell of a Ghost Dog that runs at the head of the pack. They are afraid of it because it is more cunning than they are. They tell of hunters who fail to return to camp. They are found lying dead, surrounded by wolf prints in the snow that are larger than any wolf's. And in the winter there is a certain valley they never enter because it is where the Evil Spirit chooses to dwell.

In the summer there is another visitor nobody has ever seen. It is a great, gloriously coated wolf who is unlike all others. He walks alone to an open space among the trees, where a sparkling stream of yellow nuggets, spilled from rotting moosehide sacks, slowly vanish

into the soil. He sits silently by, and then, with a single, mournful howl, departs.

He is not always alone. On long winter nights when wolves hunt meat deep into the lower valleys, he can be seen at the head of the pack. A giant among the others, his throat is filled with the song of the pack.

THE END

ABOUT THE AUTHOR

Jack London was born on January 12, 1876, in San Francisco, California. As a child, he lived on ranches and spent time on the waters of San Francisco Bay. Then, in his teens, he went to sea and became an oyster pirate.

After working odd jobs and getting into trouble with the law, Jack London began to value education. Studying very hard, he tried to cram both a high school and college education into just a few months.

Then, gold was discovered in the Klondike River valley, located in the Yukon Territory of Canada. Twenty-one-year-old London hiked there from California to find his fortune. But after spending a very cold winter in the far North without finding any gold, he decided to return to San Francisco and take up writing.

The best-known writer of his time, Jack London produced many adventure stories and novels, including *The Call of the Wild*, *The Sea-Wolf*, and *White Fang*.

Adventures of Huckleberry Finn
The Adventures of Robin Hood
The Adventures of Sherlock Holmes
The Adventures of Tom Sawyer
Alice in Wonderland
Anne of Green Gables
Black Beauty
The Call of the Wild
Gulliver's Travels
Heidi
Jane Eyre
The Legend of Sleepy Hollow
& Rip Van Winkle
A Little Princess
Little Women
Moby Dick
Oliver Twist
Peter Pan
Rebecca of Sunnybrook Farm
Robinson Crusoe
The Secret Garden
Swiss Family Robinson
Treasure Island
20,000 Leagues Under the Sea
The Wizard of Oz